THE AR[MY]
OF
HEROBRINE

AN UNOFFICIAL OVERWORLD ADVENTURE, BOOK FIVE

THE ARMIES OF HEROBRINE

DANICA DAVIDSON

Sky Pony Press
New York

Sky Pony Press books may be purchased in bulk at special discounts for
sales promotion, corporate gifts, fund-raising, or educational purposes.
Special editions can also be created to specifications. For details, contact
the Special Sales Department, Sky Pony Press, 307 West 36th Street,
11th Floor, New York, NY 10018 or info@skyhorsepublishing.com.

Sky Pony® is a registered trademark of Skyhorse Publishing, Inc.®,
a Delaware corporation.

Visit our website at www.skyponypress.com.

10 9 8 7 6 5 4 3 2 1

Library of Congress Cataloging-in-Publication Data is available on file.

Cover design by Brian Peterson
Cover artwork by Lordwhitebear

Print ISBN: 978-1-5107-1620-9
Ebook ISBN: 978-1-5107-1622-3

Printed in Canada

THE ARMIES OF HEROBRINE

CHAPTER 1

I WAS IN A DARK ROOM, SURROUNDED BY MONSTERS. To my left I saw skeletons, their bones gleaming in the darkness. To my right I saw a group of vampires with red on their mouths. The rest of the room was full of different types of ghouls, all of them pressed close together.

My hand went automatically to my diamond sword. But before I could draw it, my best friend Maison exclaimed, "No, Stevie! They're just costumes!"

I blinked. We had just entered the Halloween party at Maison's middle school. Red and orange lights were moving around the room, giving it an eerie feeling, and music was pulsing from the walls. Tables were decorated with angry-looking Jack o' Lanterns, and people were eating colorful worms and drinking out of a giant cauldron. There was a little stage set up close to the entrance where some people were dancing, but mostly the people were fighting with one another. It didn't look like any party *I* had ever seen.

"Are you sure they're costumes?" I asked. This room was spooking me so much that I didn't want to lower my sword, just in case. "These aren't servants of Herobrine?"

"This is what we do here on Earth," Yancy said. Yancy was my former enemy, current friend. "On October 31st in the Overworld, mobs are more likely to spawn with Jack o' Lanterns on their heads. On Earth, we celebrate Halloween by dressing up, having parties, eating gummy worms, and drinking punch from cauldrons. You know, we have fun."

Destiny, Yancy's cousin, could see I still wasn't convinced. "They're not servants of Herobrine," she said.

"Who cares about having fun right now?" my cousin Alex scoffed. "We have a much bigger problem on our hands."

That problem was Herobrine, the greatest mob the Overworld had ever seen. After turning the Overworld into an angry and crime-riddled place, he'd jumped through a portal to Earth, wanting to take it over and destroy it. While he was at it, he'd brainwashed everyone he could, turning them against one another. That portal, by the way, was a special one, the only one to take people back and forth from the Overworld and Earth. Maison had accidentally created it and I'd been the first person to discover how it worked.

Herobrine had even kidnapped my own dad, Steve, and made him second-in-command for the Earth takeover. At the moment we didn't know where Dad was. We *had* been able to un-brainwash Alex's mom, my Aunt Alexandra. Because Aunt Alexandra was a powerful and well-respected mayor, she was off collecting the armies of the Overworld to help us fight Herobrine.

But we had no idea when she'd be back or what sort of armies Herobrine would have collected for himself. Right now, there were five of us here to fight against Herobrine. I was an eleven-year-old boy from the Overworld and I was here with my friends Maison, Destiny, and Yancy, and my cousin, Alex. Five kids against a mob straight out of our nightmares.

"We shouldn't even be at this stupid party," Alex said grouchily. "Herobrine is planning to march on us, and we don't have plans!"

I felt sick, knowing she was right. How were we going to defeat Herobrine, especially if Aunt Alexandra didn't make it back in time?

The thing was, the five of us had been in Maison's bedroom half an hour ago, starting to make plans to fight Herobrine. But before we could do anything, Maison's mom burst into the room. Alex and I had both gone totally still in fear, because we were from the Overworld and Maison's mom didn't know about us.

However, instead of gawking at two square-looking people, Maison's mom started acting like everyone Herobrine's power had affected. She was yelling at us, telling us to get to the school Halloween party, because she hadn't spent all that money on Maison's Halloween baseball uniform costume for it to go to waste. Things that might have been a little annoying before now seemed like the end of the world to her, thanks to Herobrine's influence, and she was furious.

Trying to tell Maison's mom that the end of the world really *might* be coming didn't work, as you might imagine.

And so here we were, standing in the middle of this crazy Earth party with people eating worms made of gummies, of all things. If I hadn't been so worried about Herobrine, I would have thought this party was pretty funny.

Well, maybe not *that* funny. Like Maison's mom, the people in this room were angry and arguing with one another. One kid took a Jack o' Lantern and threw it at another kid. A teacher was screaming at someone. I hadn't just been scared by the costumes when I first walked in here—I'd been scared by the hate. It might sound weird, but you could actually feel the hate in the air. That was the power of Herobrine.

Yancy was fiddling around on his cell phone, still trying to do Herobrine research. "The Internet is back up," Yancy said, since Herobrine had been causing the Internet to go on and off throughout the day. Herobrine had also been taking over the Internet now and then to stream scary messages to all the people of Earth, telling them he would destroy them soon. The media thought it was all a prank and didn't think Earth had anything to worry about. We knew better, of course.

As Yancy fiddled with his phone, I saw his face go very pale.

"What's going on?" I demanded, heart pounding. I knew it had to be something bad.

Slowly Yancy lowered his cell phone so we could all see. Scene after scene was flashing over the cell phone, as if it were a super-fast movie. I was seeing cities and landscapes, all of them on Earth. And in every single one sat a portal to the Overworld, glowing.

"We haven't opened any more portals!" I said, feeling chilled all over.

But there was no doubt in my mind who had.

The scenes stopped flashing and a news program came on. A man in a suit was staring out at us, saying, "Thank you for joining us for the evening news. As you might have noticed, people around the world have been having difficulty connecting to the Internet during portions of the day. All of this started after the so-called 'Herobrine video,' in which a digital man referring to himself as 'Herobrine' threatened to destroy the world. Officials are calling this an elaborate Halloween prank, but it seems the prank may not be over."

Now the news program began to show some of the same scenes of Earth cities with portals in them. The newsman's voice continued over the pictures, "Strange portals have abruptly appeared in major cities across the globe. Our viewers continue to send us pictures from where they live. Here you can see portals appearing in London, Tokyo, and New York City."

The news flashed to another man, giving an interview. He seemed to be one of the "officials" the newsman had talked about.

"We're well aware of the situation," the official was saying. He looked a little nervous but very confused. "We are currently investigating, and as with the Herobrine video, we believe it is all part of a sophisticated Halloween prank. I'll take no further questions at this time."

The footage returned to the newsman. "While the portals have some people spooked, officials tell us they don't believe there is anything to worry about," he said.

"Not something to worry about!" Alex said. "Herobrine's going to send out mobs from the Overworld to Earth with these portals!"

"There's a news van out front," Destiny said. "Maybe we could warn them."

"Why would there be a news van at a Halloween party?" Maison asked

"Who cares?" Yancy said. "We have to warn the people of Earth about what's really happening."

It wasn't going to be that easy, though. As soon as I turned to follow the others outside, four green zombie arms grabbed me and slammed me back against the wall.

CHAPTER 2

"WELL, WELL, WELL," ONE ZOMBIE SAID TO the other. "What do we have here, Dirk?"

The other zombie was smirking. "I don't know, Mitch. Is it our little Stevie?"

I was pinned back against the wall, my mouth hanging open. I couldn't believe what I was seeing.

"Dirk?" I said. "Mitch? You remember me, right? Maison and I saved you from zombies earlier this year!"

Dirk and Mitch were eighth graders who used to bully Maison, but after she and I saved this middle school from a zombie attack at the beginning of the school year, Maison said Dirk and Mitch had stopped bullying and turned over a new leaf. It had taken me a minute to realize that Dirk and Mitch weren't really zombies. They were just dressed up like them. (The fact that they both smelled bad sure helped make it more realistic, though.)

I looked from one creepy grinning face to the other. If they'd changed, I couldn't tell.

"I don't remember anything about you saving us," Dirk said.

Mitch laughed. "Me neither. But I got a question for you, Stevie: Trick or treat?"

"Huh?" I said, not following. I was frantically looking for the others. They must have all gotten out the door before I could. Then I saw Maison running back over—she must have gone outside and then realized I wasn't with the others.

"Mitch! Dirk!" Maison exclaimed. "Leave Stevie alone!"

"I just want him to answer one question," Dirk said, grinding his fist into my shirt so I couldn't move. "What is it, Stevie? Trick or treat?"

I shook my head.

"He's not from here," Maison said. "He doesn't know about Halloween."

"Oh, boy!" Mitch said. "Then we get to teach him."

"Listen up, blockhead," Dirk said. "There are two things about Halloween: candy and tricks. And scary things."

"Those are three things," I said. I couldn't help it, especially after he called me "blockhead." In the Overworld everyone had blocky heads, but in this world telling someone they had a block head was an insult for some reason.

The bullies glared at me.

"On Halloween, you get to pull tricks on one another," Mitch said. "That's why we're here."

"We're also here because of the candy," Dirk said.

"I was getting to that," Mitch said, annoyed. "Whoever wins the school costume contest gets *tons* of candy for a prize. With a clever idea like zombie costumes, we're sure to win."

I glanced around. "I don't know," I said. "I see a lot of people dressed as zombies."

It was true: Zombies seemed like a popular costume at this Halloween party. I'd seen enough zombies in my life to never want to dress up like them for fun, thank you very much.

Dirk and Mitch scowled harder. "Be quiet, blockhead," Dirk said. "Or you'll find yourself attached to the flagpole by your underwear."

"We could also give him a swirly," Mitch suggested brightly.

"Nah, his head wouldn't fit in the toilet," Dirk said, as if he'd really thought about this.

"The thing is," Mitch said, "that Halloween is for babies. We're too old to be scared by it. Halloween isn't fun when it's not scary, but that's okay. Now we have a fun time scaring other kids."

"You're going to have the worst night of your life," Dirk said, a grin splitting up his green face.

I believed him, but not for the reason he thought.

"You guys really need to let me go," I said, struggling unsuccessfully to get loose. Dirk and Mitch might not have been the brightest, but they were both stronger than me. "Really, I need to get with the others before Halloween really *does* turn scary."

They both laughed uproariously. But their laughter turned to screams when someone grabbed them.

CHAPTER 3

YANCY HAD RETURNED AND SLAMMED HIS HANDS down on Dirk and Mitch's shoulders, startling them. They both jumped back and let me go.

"Hey, what's it to you?" Dirk demanded, eyeing Yancy up and down. "If you're here to get the candy, it won't work. Our costumes are way better than yours."

This was an especially dumb thing to say because Yancy wasn't even *wearing* a costume. Maison had on her baseball uniform and was holding a bat, Destiny had on a lacy black dress, and Alex and I were pretending our real bodies were our costumes—or at least, that's what Maison told us to say in case anyone asked why we looked the way we did. When Destiny had asked Yancy earlier what he was for Halloween, Yancy replied, "A surly teenager." I think he was joking, because he was just dressed as himself.

"I'm not here for the candy," Yancy said. "And by the way, I made a better zombie than you ever did."

That *was* a really good line, even though it went over Dirk and Mitch's heads. Yancy and Destiny had once turned into zombies while they were in the Overworld, and they learned that people from Earth who were bitten by zombies became zombies but still managed to keep their minds. They even had the power to tell normal zombies what to do.

"No, our zombie costumes are the best ever," Mitch argued. "Do you know why we're so believable as zombies?"

"Because you don't have any brains?" Yancy offered.

It took them a second, but when they got it, it made them mad. I think the only reason they weren't charging Yancy like they'd charged me was because Yancy was older and bigger than them. Eighth graders got a lot less all-powerful next to twelfth graders.

"We're going to get you!" Dirk threatened. "You and Maison and Stevie and Destiny and—who are you?" He was distracted by Alex, who'd just joined us.

The next thing Dirk knew, he had an arrow pointed at his chest. Alex didn't mess around with her bow and arrows. "I'm the best shot under twelve in the Overworld," Alex said. "Want to test me?"

"Um, hey, look over there," Mitch said. We didn't look, but he and Dirk still took the opportunity to hightail it out of there and hide among the crowd.

Yancy shook his head in disgust. "Let's get back to the news van," he said.

When we stepped outdoors, I saw that twilight was falling and the street lamps were all coming on. Before long, it would be completely dark. A big van with some sort of giant oval jutting out from the top was parked under the glare of a street lamp, near the middle school. Standing next to the van were a man and woman. The man was holding some heavy equipment on his shoulder that I guessed was a camera, though it was much bigger than the cameras Maison had shown me. The blond woman beside him was holding a microphone and her hair was so done up that it reminded me of cotton candy. But there was also something very familiar about this woman . . .

"I know her!" Maison cried. "She's the woman who interviewed me for the news after the school had the zombie attack!"

Maison obviously remembered the woman's name, too, because she ran over, shouting, "Lilac Waters! Lilac! Ms. Waters! We need to talk to you!"

Lilac was fiddling with something by her ear and then turned her attention our way. Her name reminded me of the lilacs in the Overworld, which got me thinking about how much I missed home. And how I couldn't go home until Herobrine was defeated . . . *if* we could defeat him.

"I remember you," Lilac said. "Maison, right?"

"We have to talk to you about the Herobrine messages," Maison said. "And all the portals showing up around the world!"

The woman sighed. "Oh, those things? I told my boss I wanted to do a story on it, because it made me think of the zombie attack your school had. But do you know what my boss said? He said the story was just some prank and wasn't 'hard news.' So that was the end of that."

"Wasn't 'hard news'?" Yancy cried. "Everyone's computer was taken over by someone threatening to destroy the world! And how do you explain all those portals?"

"Well, no one can actually destroy the whole world," she said with a dark little chuckle, like she thought we were being ridiculous. "I mean, how would they even go about it? The portals, well, I'm sure there's a logical explanation."

We exchanged grim looks. Herobrine had powers beyond anything a person on Earth would understand. He had entered my nightmares to tell me about his plans, he could teleport through the air, and he was wreaking havoc through this world's technology. Who knew what else he had up his sleeve?

"Then why are you here?" Maison said.

The woman sighed again. "Because my boss said everyone seems angry and jumpy, and he wanted me to get a 'feel-good' story to cheer people up. So I'm here to do a story on who wins the middle school costume contest." She pointed at Alex and me. "I think you two have a good shot at winning. You really look like those *Minecraft* characters."

"What if we have details about the Herobrine story that we can share?" Destiny said.

This intrigued her. "Like what?"

"Like that you're right: There's a connection between Herobrine and the school attack before," Maison said. "Those zombies came through a portal from the *Minecraft* world, and so did Herobrine. Except those zombies were mindless monsters and just attacked the school because they found it. Herobrine is way smarter, and he wants to ruin everything."

Lilac's eyebrows jumped up her forehead. "That's quite a story," she said, sounding skeptical.

I had started to get excited because she was listening to us. Now I got worried. How were we going to convince her?

"You see this?" Yancy said, holding out his cell phone. "This is how Herobrine got out. He got on my game here and jumped out . . . ."

"Okay, kids, okay," she said. "Your story is very cute, but I need solid proof or my boss will laugh me out of town. After he fires me. You kids should go enjoy the punch inside. I need to get to work."

She turned and talked with the man who had the camera, already over what we'd said.

"Ms. Waters!" Maison tried again, "We need—"

Lilac turned back to us, her eyes flashing with sudden, cold anger. "I said I have to get back to work!" she snapped. Herobrine's abrupt power over her was unmistakable. We slowly backed away.

"I knew it was too good to be true, that she was being nice to us at first," Yancy muttered. "I've met a few people today who are still acting nice, but then they start to get meaner and meaner. Sometimes they snap out of it for a bit, but then they get cruel again."

Maison and Destiny nodded sadly, as if they'd experienced the same thing with people.

That wasn't the only thing that had me upset about this meeting with Lilac, though: It stung that she called us "kids." I knew what that meant. She didn't think kids could do anything that important.

I looked at the four people with me. In the Overworld, we'd found music discs that had prophesied we'd be the five to defeat Herobrine, if anyone could defeat him. We'd been the only people to hear those music discs while everyone else in the Overworld was falling under Herobrine's spell.

We were a ragtag group of people from two different worlds, with very different backgrounds. But we didn't have any special powers, like Herobrine. We didn't have people believing us when we were trying to warn them of the danger they were in.

And like Lilac said, we were just kids.

I had one of the music discs in my toolkit, and I took it out and shook it. Unfortunately, now that we knew Herobrine was close, the music discs had gone silent. Right when we needed those clues the most.

"We need help!" I said. "Why are you so quiet now?"

The music disc was as silent as ever, but I heard a familiar voice gasp, "Stevie?"

CHAPTER 4

I T WAS DEFINITELY A NIGHT FOR SEEING OLD FACES. I turned and there was Ms. Reid, Maison's shop class teacher. Ms. Reid had been there the day of the zombie attack, and she'd helped us fight back.

Right now Ms. Reid wasn't looking mad, unlike just about everyone else we'd seen. She looked worried. And very interested in me.

Ms. Reid beckoned us away from Lilac and the news van. "What are you doing here, Stevie?" Ms. Reid whispered.

She looked like a sympathetic listener, and before I knew it, I spilled everything, with Yancy and Maison backing me up. Destiny and Alex mostly watched and listened. I pushed the music disc back into my toolkit, thinking Ms. Reid might be a better help right now.

When I was done, Ms. Reid sucked in a deep breath. "I knew it!" she said. "That news reporter Lilac never saw the zombie attack. But I did, and it made me a believer. And I had a feeling that wouldn't be the end of it. Oh, I told the PTA that there was probably going to be a zombie apocalypse and we needed to be prepared, but they didn't believe me!"

"Will you help us, Ms. Reid?" Maison asked.

She nodded. "I don't know the rules of *Minecraft* like you do, though," she said. "I need your directions. But first I need to go get us some stuff from the shop class room that might be helpful."

She started to head back into the school. Unfortunately, Mitch and Dirk barreled out the door, fighting with some other kids, and she had to go take care of that first.

"I wonder what she has in the shop class room," Destiny said.

"She looks pretty preoccupied," Maison noted, watching as Ms. Reid was trying to physically drag Dirk off some other kid. "Maybe we should go ahead there and wait for her. Going through the party will be the fastest way."

When we stepped inside, the music seemed even louder. It was singing something about the Monster Mash, whatever that was. A screen was pulled down across one wall and was playing some kind of scary movie with fake-looking zombies and screaming people, but the kids weren't paying much attention to it. More fights were going on and more people were throwing Jack o' Lanterns.

As we tried to walk through the room, people were shoving against us and yelling. It was making me so mad that I almost shoved back. I wanted to yell, "Can't you see we're trying to do something important here?" I swallowed the words down. Being pushed around was annoying, but my anger was so strong that I had a feeling it was Herobrine getting to me. I couldn't let him do that. Someone shoved Alex so hard that she fell down. Her hands immediately went to her arrows, then stopped. Like me, she'd almost just reacted out of anger.

"This place is a mess," Yancy muttered as I helped Alex back up. "Halloween is supposed to be scary, but it's supposed to be fun-scary."

A brawl started in front of us, with two kids really going at it. Ms. Reid had to rush over and pull them apart now, too.

"What's wrong with you kids?" Ms. Reid shouted, her face gone nasty with anger. I tensed up. I didn't want Ms. Reid falling under Herobrine's spell, too! Did this mean she was no longer going to help us?

"My mom needs to get here with her Overworld armies soon," Alex said. "Until then, maybe we should go to where all these portals are and try to warn the people. Earth isn't that big, is it?"

When she saw the depressed looks on Yancy, Destiny, and Maison's faces, she clammed up.

Right then, a very loud noise exploded from Yancy's pocket. Even in the midst of all the yelling, screaming, music, and movie sounds, the noise was so loud that we all jumped.

Yancy pulled his cell phone out of his pocket, confused. The glow of the cell phone lit up Yancy's face, making it glow luridly in the middle of all the orange and red flashing lights. Despite all the strange shades reflecting on his skin, I could still see his face immediately drain of all color.

"What is it?" Alex demanded.

Slowly Yancy lowered his cell phone so we could all see.

"What's going on, Yancy?" Destiny asked, frightened. "What did you press to get the phone to say that?"

"I didn't press anything!" Yancy said.

Block letters slowly filtered across the screen. It was the same handwriting Herobrine had used in signs he'd left for us around the Overworld.

TURN AROUND, it said.

CHAPTER 5

CRINGING, WE TURNED TO FACE THE ENTRANCE, and the stage. Standing on the stage was a giant portal with mists swirling out from its bottom like smoke. It hadn't been there seconds before.

"He knows we're here," I gasped.

The big screen playing the scary movie had changed. It was now playing scenes of portals all over Earth. The portals also had the smoke-like wisps of mist curling around the bottom like a spooky threat. Portals in the Overworld didn't have mist like that.

And we weren't the only ones to notice the change. Slowly, the other kids stopped arguing and attacking one another and looked at the movie screen and the portal on stage.

Suddenly, all the lights went out! Kids started to scream, this time in terror. Except for the glowing portal, the room was nothing but darkness.

Just as quickly, the movie screen began working again. A few lights snapped back on, but it was only the red lights, casting a frightening glow over everyone's features.

Herobrine's face was on the giant movie screen.

"Happy Halloween," Herobrine said with menacing, evil politeness. His smile was almost a sneer. "I think I heard someone earlier saying that Halloween was just for babies, and it wasn't scary anymore."

"Yeah!" Mitch cheered out of the crowd. "You got that right!"

"Oh, don't worry," Herobrine said, that terrible smile growing even bigger, even colder. "I've been treating you long enough. I think it's time that we had a little trick. Are you all ready for my grand entrance?"

I clutched my sword. He was still milking it, enjoying the torture of keeping us uncertain. I burst out, "Stop it, Herobrine! Stop hiding and show yourself!"

Even without pupils, I felt it when Herobrine's enormous white eyes sought me out. "Stevie," he purred with pretend fondness. "If you insist, I'll be right there."

The red lights all rushed to highlight the glowing portal. The movie screen went blank.

"He's coming out of the portal!" I cried.

Immediately my friends and I tried to run for the portal, only to find we couldn't get to it. All the kids and teachers were stuck in place, as if they were frozen in a nightmare. I could see them blinking and turning their heads, their faces filled with fear, but their feet stayed planted on the ground. We were running into people and they couldn't move out of our way.

"Look!" someone said.

When I looked back at the stage, I found myself frozen, too. The whole room felt icy cold as a leg slowly emerged from the portal. There was a crunch as the large foot came soundly down on the stage. Another foot emerged, and out of the glowing portal loomed the rest of Herobrine's body. He seemed even taller than I remembered, stepping right out in the open there, daring us to do anything to stop him.

If the people in here knew what was good for them, they'd be running away, screaming. They wouldn't be caught standing there, staring at the very being who promised to destroy them all.

Then I heard someone manage to cry, "His eyes!"

Normally you could look at someone's eyes and get a feeling for what they were thinking. When I looked into the depths of Herobrine's eyes, I couldn't get his thoughts, but I could feel his evil, and it made me want to cry out.

This was a being who lived only for destruction. This was a being with no sympathy or understanding. Real people could do good and bad things. Herobrine had only hatred because he'd been created by a cyber-bully, so hatred was the core of him.

In his hand he held a diamond sword, the most powerful kind of sword you could have in the Overworld. On his face, he had a terrible smile.

"My name is Herobrine," he told the rapt audience. "And tonight is your last night on Earth."

CHAPTER 6

O FAIR!" MITCH SHOUTED FROM THE CROWD. "He's going to win the costume contest for sure!"

"Yeah!" Dirk complained loudly. "He got to use special effects! That's cheating!"

Herobrine turned his sickly smile toward Mitch and Dirk, who were close to the front of the crowd. "I'm not interested in your costume contest," Herobrine said. "But there is something I'd like you to see. Do you enjoy scary movies?"

Mitch and Dirk whooped, which I guess was a yes. Everyone else couldn't even move, let alone talk.

Herobrine pointed to the screen on the wall, which was still showing cities with portals. "Then I'd like to call your attention to this new film."

Heads turned. Mitch complained, "That's just a bunch of cities! Where's that zombie movie from earlier?"

"Oh?" Herobrine looked beside himself with excitement. "Keep watching."

On the screen, zombies began to come out of the portal.

"No!" I realized it was my own voice that broke out. As I watched, zombies approached unsuspecting people who were out trick-or-treating in their Halloween costumes. The people really seemed to believe that this was just a prank.

One zombie approached a man who'd stopped to take a picture with his phone, laughing. I wanted to shout at the man to get away, but of course this film was happening somewhere else and he'd never hear me.

The man's laughter turned to shrieks as one zombie grabbed him and sank his teeth into the man. The man was screaming and screaming. The zombie threw him to the ground, done with him, and the man cried out as his skin turned green and zombie features came over his face.

"Cool!" Mitch said.

"It looks so real!" Dirk said. "This is way better than the zombie movie they were playing earlier!"

Herobrine smiled with pride.

"That's sick!" Yancy said in a low voice, as if he couldn't bear to talk louder. I saw that Destiny was struggling not to cry.

"Those people don't know how to protect themselves!" Destiny whimpered.

No, they didn't—that was clear from the video that was still playing. Seeing what had happened to the man, all the people nearby began running as fast as they could, zombies at their heels. One zombie grabbed a woman and—

The screen flashed to another scene, in a different city. The people here were speaking in a language I didn't recognize, and they were laughing with delight as they saw the first zombies come out of the portal in front of them. It was a repeat of the last time. People were taking pictures, then getting attacked. The lucky ones managed to escape . . . for now. The ones caught off guard were seized and bitten by the zombies. One by one, Herobrine was starting to turn every person on Earth into a zombie.

Then the screen split into a bunch of different scenes. Twenty different shots showed twenty different portals with emerging zombies. The zombies moaned and staggered, hunting their prey. Twenty scenes of kids and adults running for their lives, trying to stay out of the clutches of monsters. Some of them tried to run in one direction, only for zombies to pop out in front of them, blocking them off. They didn't stand a chance.

"What do you think?" Herobrine asked. "Is this scary enough for you?"

"It's okay," Dirk said with a shrug.

The red lights blared over Herobrine's face, making his white eyes turn the color of blood. "I can make it scarier," he offered.

Immediately, zombies began to emerge from the portal on the stage, lurching toward everyone at the party.

CHAPTER 7

THE NEAR-TOTAL SILENCE TURNED TO SCREAMS AS kids and teachers tried to make a beeline out of the room and outdoors to safety. Mitch and Dirk let out the highest shrieks of all and fell down to the floor in terror, holding their arms over their heads in protection.

"Not this again!" Mitch wailed.

"I hate zombies!" Dirk cried.

With the rush of people, I found a path through the crowd. I dashed toward the stage, my sword at the ready.

"Herobrine!" I yelled. "Stop this now!"

Maison and Alex were right at my heels. When a zombie reared up before us, Maison hurled her baseball bat at it, knocking it away. Alex had her bow and arrows at the ready, shooting zombies as fast as she could. She was hitting them moments before they reached students, saving the kids just in the nick of time.

But more and more zombies kept coming out of the portal, and Alex only had so many arrows.

I leapt onto the stage, my sword out. Herobrine laughed.

"A diamond sword?" Herobrine said. "You think you can defeat me with that little thing?"

"We will defeat you!" I promised, rushing at him with the sword. I thought he might disappear on me, but instead he simply raised his diamond sword, blocking me. He did it so easily that he had time to yawn and stretch before I could recover to attack again.

"You have a diamond sword and I have a diamond sword," Herobrine said. "Do you think we're evenly matched?"

Without waiting for me to answer, he went on, "Of course, I also have power over the Overworld, the Nether, and now Earth as well. You don't have any of those things, do you, Stevie?"

"Earth is not going to sit back and let you destroy it!" I said.

He laughed again, as if my words really cracked him up. "Earth people don't know how to fight zombies," he sneered. "You saw for yourself. The Overworld already bows before me and calls me its master. It won't be long before I have Earth as well."

Maison was battling through the zombies, swinging her baseball bat in every direction. When she managed to get onstage, Maison shouted to the audience, "I need your attention! This is just like the time we had the mob attack in the auditorium! Grab whatever you can use for weapons and hit back at the zombies."

The kids instantly ran to obey. Earlier they couldn't get along, but with a zombie army at their heels, they saw they couldn't be bickering if they wanted to stay safe. Kids were hitting back at zombies with Jack o' Lanterns, decorations, even parts of their Halloween costumes. Someone knocked over the cauldron of punch and the zombies slipped in the liquid, falling before they could hurt anyone. Out of the corner of my eye I could see Alex's arrows continue to fly, taking out zombies right and left.

"I'm just giving the kids what they asked for," Herobrine said to me with a shrug. "They wanted something scary."

"Don't play dumb!" I said, slashing out with my sword. Herobrine jumped back, missing my slashes. "You know that's not what they meant!"

"People deserve this, Stevie," Herobrine said. "Whether it's the Overworld or Earth, it's all the same. People cheat, people lie, people hurt others. I'm only taking what they already do and repeating it on a much larger scale. I'd say fair is fair."

Was he really that sick in the head? "People also help one another!" I said. My sword slammed against his but I couldn't push him back. He was too strong. "They also come together!"

"You think the whole Earth will come together over this?" Herobrine scoffed. "People fight too much to know what's good for them."

He pushed back, knocking me down. I fell with a grunt. Herobrine stepped up close, looming over me, his diamond sword pointed right to my face.

Wait. No . . . .

"Notice something?" Herobrine asked.

I jumped back up at him with a roar. "You monster!" I shouted. "That's my dad's diamond sword!"

"So it is!" Herobrine beamed.

I was seeing red, and not just because of the lights. I felt my rage boil up in me. That diamond sword was my dad's prized possession, and he never let anyone use it. How dare Herobrine steal it for his evil gains!

"Give back my dad!" I yelled. "I know you have him!"

"Indeed I do," Herobrine said. "But the question for you is, where? Is he on Earth? In the Overworld? In the Nether? Where do you think I've stashed him away, Stevie?"

I was so overcome with fury that all I could do was charge at Herobrine, screaming. In the background I could hear Maison shouting to people, telling them what to do. I could hear Alex's arrows shooting through the air. The moan of zombies. The cries of scared people. Mitch and Dirk huddling and whimpering on the ground. All of it sounded far away to me, because my whole world had really just become Herobrine and me. This was it. I was going to take him out.

I drew back my sword and sent it flying. And as soon as it hit Herobrine, he disappeared.

CHAPTER 8

FOR A MOMENT I STOOD THERE, PANTING. WHERE had he gone? I picked up my sword and looked frantically around the room. It was a crazy scene, filled with fighting kids and attacking zombies. But no Herobrine. He had disappeared when he had me at the most angry. Maybe he knew that teleporting right then would also make me the most vulnerable.

"Stevie!" someone shouted.

I whirled, and there was Ms. Reid running over, pulling a cart behind her. At first I thought my eyes were playing tricks on me. The cart was filled with wooden swords like the kind I made in the Overworld.

"My shop class students have been making these!" Ms. Reid hollered over the noise. She was like her old self again, wanting to be helpful. I remembered Yancy saying that some people weren't as affected by Herobrine's magic as others were, and might come back to themselves for short periods. "I've been keeping them locked up in case we ever needed them!"

"Maison!" I turned and shouted out. Maison was right up by the portal, hitting zombies as they first emerged. When she turned at the sound of her name, her face lit up at Ms. Reid's cart of swords.

"Everyone!" Maison yelled to the crowds. "Grab a wooden sword!"

There was almost a stampede as kids ran to get the wooden swords. A few kids accidentally stepped on Dirk and Mitch in their rush.

"Hey, quit it!" Dirk shouted, but still didn't get up to grab a weapon or protect himself.

"Yeah! We're trying to hide here!" Mitch said.

Ms. Reid was handing the wooden swords out as fast as she could. Would there be enough swords to stop all these zombies?

And then it hit me. If I could destroy the portal here, that would prevent any more zombies from getting through! We could take out the zombies already here, and then we'd be able to figure out how to help everyone else!

"Alex!" I called. "We need to destroy the portal!"

Alex heard me and nodded. She yanked her pickaxe out of her toolkit and the two of us charged straight to the portal.

I hit one of the portal's stones with my sword, using all my might. At the same moment, Alex struck another stone with her pickaxe.

It should have been the perfect plan. Cut off the source of the zombies and get some relief.

But of course Herobrine would never let it be that easy. Hitting against the portal was like hitting an electric current of redstones. Alex and I each yelped out in pain, and we fell back. The portal continued to stand there, completely undamaged. And the zombies continued to march out, one after another.

One of the emerging zombies hulked over me, its mouth open in a moan, its hands reaching out. Right before it seized me, Maison jumped in the way and struck it with her baseball bat. The zombie vanished.

"Is there no way to break the portal?" Maison exclaimed as she helped me back up. Alex was already back up on her feet, though she looked dizzy from the fall.

"It's Herobrine's dark magic," Alex said angrily.

Yancy and Destiny hurried onto the stage with us.

"Whoa, Stevie, are you okay?" Yancy asked.

Before I could answer, I heard Herobrine call from above, "You're not the only one to make special portals, Stevie."

My head flew up. There was Herobrine, floating straight above us! I clutched my sword and yelled, "What are you doing? Can't you see how many people you're hurting?"

It was a stupid argument, because of course Herobrine knew exactly how many people he was hurting, and he didn't care. I was used to being able to reason with people.

"Yes, I can see quite clearly," Herobrine said, gesturing grandly toward the movie screen. When I dared to glance at it, I saw it had twenty new scenes on it. The cities were different from the ones he was showing us before, but the carnage was the same.

Was there some way I could vault into the air and charge Herobrine? I looked around, but nothing was tall enough to get me anywhere close to where he floated overhead. Herobrine knew this, and he smiled wolfishly down at me.

Nearby, Yancy was trying to examine the portal at the same time as he was hitting at the zombies that emerged. I saw that he'd grabbed one of Ms. Reid's wooden swords and was using it as a weapon.

"There's got to be a way to break this portal!" Yancy exclaimed. "In *Minecraft*, there's always a way!"

"You think this is still *Minecraft*?" Herobrine scoffed. "If you think this is all a game, you're sorely mistaken."

Yancy struck the portal with his wooden sword and fell back in pain, just as Alex and I had done. "Ouch!" he cried out, clutching his sword arm.

I couldn't take it anymore. I charged off the stage and thrust myself as high in the air as I could, swiping at Herobrine with my sword. All around me I could hear the screams of kids and the moans and rasps of zombies.

Even though I stretched my arm out as far as it could go, my sword just narrowly missed brushing against Herobrine's feet. Now I was no longer charging—I was falling, back down to the floor, where I could see zombies waiting for me! I flailed uselessly. How could I have gotten so caught up in the moment that I would let myself do something so stupid?

A hand grabbed me.

At first I sagged in relief, thinking I was saved. But then, as I hung there in the air, I realized there was only one being who could have caught me.

Slowly, Herobrine lifted me up, tight in his clutches, until he had my face inches from his. His white eyes bored into mine, his creepy smile cracked like a broken mirror, promising misfortune.

"Well, here we are, face-to-face, Stevie," Herobrine mocked. "What are you going to do?"

CHAPTER 9

HE HAD ME TOO TIGHT IN HIS CLUTCHES TO MOVE much, and I knew that if I attacked him, he'd drop me to the floor for the waiting zombies. When I looked below, I saw an even bigger swarm of zombies had gathered, staring up at me the way my cat stared when she saw I had fresh fish. That concentration, that hunger. Those zombies weren't going anywhere until they'd devoured me.

"What do you want, Herobrine?" I asked in a begging voice. I realized I was pleading with him, trying to come up with a compromise. My mind was haunted with all the attacked people I'd seen in the videos, the people being turned into zombies against their will. So far the kids at this party had fought the zombies successfully and none of them had been turned, but I didn't know how long that would be the case.

"I'm getting exactly what I want," Herobrine replied.

"I—I'll make you a promise," I said, thinking quickly. "Let everyone go. Take the portals away and stop the zombies. Release my dad. If you do, I'll—I'll . . ."

I swallowed, the words not wanting to come out. "I'll let you have me as a prisoner," I said.

I could tell Herobrine wasn't expecting this. It startled him for a moment, then he began to laugh.

"Well, aren't you noble," he scoffed. "But do you really think I want one measly kid when I can have all the worlds bow before me?"

"Think about it!" I went on. "I'm the boy with the portal, right? I'm the one who stopped the zombie takeover of the Overworld. Wouldn't you feel proud to say you'd captured me and held me prisoner?"

I didn't even know what I was saying. I just knew I had to save the others, and if it meant me spending the rest of my life as a prisoner of Herobrine, that was still better than the fate of living free but knowing how many people he'd hurt.

But Herobrine was right. Even though I was trying to make myself sound really impressive, I knew I really wasn't. I'd only been able to save the special portal and stop the zombie takeover because of the help of others. By myself, I really was just a measly, eleven-year-old kid, wasn't I?

"I'll tell you what," Herobrine said, dipping his glowing eyes closer to me. "I'll let you in on a little secret. Would you like to hear it?"

My first thought was that he was going to tell me he'd done something horrible to Dad. I couldn't bear to hear that! But I nodded, because this might be the only way to get information.

"There is a way to destroy those portals," he said.

I almost choked. Why would he tell me this? Was it just a trick?

His face loomed closer. The red lights kept passing over him like a sunset. "The only way to destroy the portals is to destroy me," he whispered.

My heart thudded. That's why he'd told me— because he was convinced we couldn't destroy him. He just wanted to rub it in.

"You've been chasing after me for a long time," Herobrine went on. "You followed music discs with prophecies, attacked me on a mountaintop, even went through the Nether so you'd be able to confront me now. But this is the end of the road, boy. I have powers you only dream of, and all you have is a puny sword and some little friends."

He had me held close, gripping my shirt in one hand. In his other hand, he raised Dad's diamond sword over my face. I saw the sharp blade's sparkle inches from my eyes.

"It's time to say goodbye," Herobrine said.

CHAPTER 10

BEFORE HEROBRINE COULD MOVE, HE LET OUT A sharp cry of pain. He looked down, and I did too, not understanding what had happened. As soon as I saw, my eyes widened. Several arrows had hit Herobrine in the leg, and Alex stood defiantly below, her loaded bow still pointed at him.

"Let Stevie go!" she hollered.

Herobrine's cheeks were flushed with red, and it wasn't from the red lights.

"You little brat!" Herobrine began.

"Put him down now!" Alex said, sending another arrow soaring. Herobrine managed to dodge this one, but I could see the ones she'd hit him with were causing him to lose some of his health. He sagged back in the air, still holding me.

"Your arrows are pitiful!" Herobrine shouted down to her. She sent another one flying his way and he dodged easily, having expected it.

"There are going to be a lot more arrows than these!" Alex said, reloading her bow.

Just like that, Herobrine dropped me.

I braced myself for the twin terrors of hitting the floor and being attacked by zombies. To my surprise, I landed in someone's arms. I realized I'd clamped my eyes shut during the fall, and when I opened them, I saw that Yancy had caught me. There was no zombie horde anymore. Maison and Destiny were slashing back at the zombies in the area, Maison with her bat and Destiny with a wooden sword. I realized that, while I was in the air, they must have cleared out the area and then had Alex shoot Herobrine with her arrows so he'd let me go.

Without a word, Yancy set me down on my feet. Alex and Herobrine continued to yell at each other, him in the air and her on the stage.

"I'm going to get you for that!" Herobrine threatened.

"No, we're going to get you!" Alex answered. "Because you just told us how to close all these portals, and we have a way to defeat you."

Herobrine sneered down at her. "And why do you think that?"

"You thought you brainwashed everyone in the Overworld," Alex said heatedly. "But I un-brain-washed my mom, and she's off right now, collecting all the armies of the Overworld! The people on Earth might not know how to fight zombies, but these warriors will!"

She was trying to scare Herobrine. So when he smiled at her as if she'd said something really funny, my insides went cold.

"Is that so?" Herobrine said.

"Yes!" Alex said. "She'll bring millions of soldiers, and then we'll no longer be outnumbered! I'd love to see the look on your face when she shows up with her armies!"

Herobrine disappeared out of the air and reappeared a moment later, standing on the stage. He was a few feet away from Alex and right next to the portal, so close he could touch it.

No one was coming out of the portal. After all those rushing zombies, why had they stopped?

Wait.

A foot came out. I tensed, holding up my sword, then realized it wasn't a zombie's foot. It was the square foot of someone from the Overworld.

Another foot emerged. A regal woman with red hair stepped completely through the portal. In her hand she clutched a diamond sword, and her body was dressed in glinting armor. She was definitely here to do battle.

"Mom!" Alex gasped in relief. "I'm so glad you're—!"

She started to run toward Aunt Alexandra, then stopped with another gasp. This time it was a gasp of terror.

More people from the Overworld were stepping through the portal, following Aunt Alexandra. These men and women all had iron swords and were covered with armor. They were all dressed for battle, just like she was.

But they all had blank eyes, just like Herobrine. When Aunt Alexandra looked out at the crowd, the whiteness of her eyes gleamed in the scary lights, her pupils gone. She bowed before Herobrine, offering her diamond sword for him to take.

"I have brought you the armies of the Overworld, my master," she said to him. "They will obey your every word."

CHAPTER 11

"MOM, NO!" ALEX SHRIEKED. SHE TRIED TO run to her mom, realized the danger of it, and stopped short.

"It can't be," I heard Maison cry out from behind me. "Alex's mom was our best chance."

"Please, keep the sword," Herobrine told Aunt Alexandra. "You'll need it to fight with. Besides . . ." He made sure to look out over the crowd and focus his evil eyes on me. "I already have a diamond sword."

"No, no," Alex kept saying, shaking her head. "Mom, listen to me! Mom, I know you're in there!"

Aunt Alexandra turned and looked at Alex with no recognition.

"Well, Alex," Herobrine said. "You were right that your mother was bringing all the armies of the Overworld. There was one detail you missed, though." He had turned his eyes away from me and was staring at Alex with sick enjoyment.

"Did you really think you had un-brainwashed your mother?" he went on, relishing this. "Your mother has been working for me ever since I rose to power. I only had her pretend to come to her senses."

"Mom, no." Alex was whimpering now.

"Who is that girl?" Aunt Alexandra asked Herobrine, her lip curled in disgust.

"She is part of the enemy army," Herobrine replied. "As are all the other people in this world. Tell me, Mayor Alexandra, did you find the forest of portals I placed?"

She nodded.

"And are your millions of soldiers going through all the portals, to make sure they cover every inch of this globe?"

She nodded again. "I have done everything you ordered, master."

"Excellent," Herobrine said. He turned back to glare at Alex.

"Oh, Alex," he said, "I loved seeing the look on your face when your mother arrived with *my* armies."

I couldn't take it anymore. I started charging toward the stage.

"Well, Alex?" Herobrine prompted. "You say you're the best shot under age twelve in the Overworld. Aren't you going to use your arrows?"

"I'm not going to shoot my mom!" Alex cried.

Aunt Alexandra looked at Alex coldly.

"That's fine with me," Herobrine said, before telling Aunt Alexandra, "Have your troops take care of every human in the area. Don't hurt the zombies, because the zombies are on your side, too."

"Yes, master," Aunt Alexandra said.

"And take care of their leader first," Herobrine said. He pointed toward Alex. "Her."

Without a moment's hesitation, Aunt Alexandra turned on Alex with her diamond sword, slashing out. Alex jumped back and the blow missed. She had her bow and arrows out but couldn't bear to use them.

I leapt onstage and hurled my sword down, knocking it into Aunt Alexandra's sword. The blow was strong and Aunt Alexandra had been so consumed with attacking Alex that she hadn't seen me. Her sword broke through the stage floor and got caught there.

"Aunt Alexandra!" I said, even though I knew it probably wouldn't work. If her own daughter couldn't reach her, how did I have any hope? "Don't you recognize us?"

"He's another one of their leaders," Herobrine said. "Take him out, too."

Aunt Alexandra ripped her sword out of the floor, the blade sparkling. Her sword was scary, but the most terrifying thing about her were those eyes, lost and vacant under Herobrine's spell.

"Troops!" she called. "Take care of all the humans you find! Leave the leaders of this army to me."

When her sword came down, I blocked it with my own, straining. Now that Aunt Alexandra was concentrating on me, she was a lot harder to fight. I felt my feet slipping under me as I pushed with all my strength, trying to keep her sword at bay.

All around us, the Overworld troops descended on the Halloween party, raising their weapons. Kids were trying to fight them off and having no luck. Their wooden swords easily broke under the iron swords of the Overworld army. Kids were running to corners of the room to hide, followed by the troops and the zombies. In the chaos, I lost sight of Alex and my friends.

"Fantastic!" Herobrine said.

Aunt Alexandra hit me hard with her sword and I fell back, sprawling across the ground. My sword flew from my fingers, landing just out of my reach.

"It looks as if you have this all under control, Mayor Alexandra," Herobrine said. "Remember your orders. I'm off to make sure all the other attacks on Earth are going as well as this one."

With that, he vanished back through the portal. Aunt Alexandra approached me from overhead, her sword raised.

CHAPTER 12

AUNT ALEXANDRA'S SWORD FLEW THROUGH THE air. A wooden sword appeared out of nowhere just in the nick of time, blocking her.

No, wait, it wasn't a sword that had saved me. It was a bat! Maison had jumped over, blocking the sword attack. The sword sliced partway into it, but the bat stayed in one piece.

This gave me enough time to snatch my sword and get back to my feet. Aunt Alexandra looked furiously at Maison, who was not backing down.

"You're one of the leaders here, too, aren't you?" Aunt Alexandra snarled at Maison. "I recognize you."

"You recognize me because I'm on your side, against Herobrine!" Maison said.

"You're a fool!" Aunt Alexandra said, now coming at Maison with her sword. "You could have run for safety, but you come rushing to help this—this—" She didn't know what to call me. I knew it was nothing good.

"To help my friend, yes!" Maison shouted. She and I both blocked Aunt Alexandra's sword, Maison with her bat and me with my own blade.

Aunt Alexandra tried to take another step toward us, then gasped. She looked down. An arrow had caught her boot, pinning it to the stage floor without actually hurting her foot. A few feet away stood Alex, a look of defiant confidence on her face, her bow and arrow still raised. Several more of her arrows flew through the air, all of them pinning Aunt Alexandra in place by her boots without wounding her.

"I said I was the best shot in the Overworld under twelve!" Alex yelled out.

Aunt Alexandra roared in outrage and began snatching the arrows out to free herself. The arrows wouldn't keep her in place for long, but they might give us a chance to escape.

"Stevie, over here!" I heard Yancy call. I looked, and he was to the side of the stage with Destiny, gesturing frantically. I didn't need any more beckoning. Alex, Maison, and I dove off the stage, landing next to them. It was a tiny, wedged-in area, giving us just enough protection to talk. The zombies and soldiers seemed too caught up with what was in front of them to notice us here.

"Herobrine got away!" I said. I saw that Yancy was staring, wide-eyed, at something behind me, and he lifted one shaky pale finger and pointed. I turned, already feeling sick, not wanting to know what new horror I would have to see.

On the movie screen were twenty new scenes of twenty new cities. All of the portals had members of the Overworld army streaming out. Just like the troops here, these men and women were decked out with armor and iron swords. And every single one of them had the same blank, white eyes.

In each city on screen, the Overworld army immediately got to work attacking the people, chasing them into the arms of zombies. Some people were grabbed—I guessed to be taken prisoner. I didn't know what Herobrine had in mind.

And then I saw him.

Him.

Herobrine loomed over one of the portals in one of the scenes. He was cheering the troops on, telling them exactly what to do. The army, like a bunch of little Herobrines, fought and slashed and attacked with mind-numbing fury.

"I was so stupid!" Alex wailed. "I thought my mom was going to bring the armies to help us!"

"We all fell for it," Destiny said, putting a comforting hand on Alex's shoulder. "Don't feel bad."

"Herobrine left here because Stevie was weaponless on the ground, and he didn't think Alex would fight her mother," Yancy murmured, sounding as if he were in a trance. He seemed to be thinking deeply. "He thought he'd already won."

"What's that have to do with anything?" I demanded.

"I'm trying to figure out what he's intending!" Yancy said. "He's got all this stuff planned out with the zombies and the armies, but he's also making stupid mistakes."

"What do you mean?" I asked.

"You saw how Alex got him with arrows while he had you," Yancy said. "Every other weapon he's dodged. But he was just so . . . so consumed in gloating and torturing you that he let his guard down."

"You think his ego is of the key to beating him?" Destiny asked.

I looked at the carnage around me, thinking nothing could possibly end this.

"We don't have time to stop and think!" I snapped at Yancy. I was watching Aunt Alexandra struggling to get loose from her arrows. She'd almost made it, and then she'd probably come back after us.

On the screen, Herobrine was leaping from portal to portal around the world, celebrating and urging the troops on. A few times he seemed to grin and wink our way, as if he knew we were watching him.

"I have an idea," Yancy said. "I'm going to even the odds here."

"How?" Maison asked, as confused as I was.

Yancy smiled. "We have to make me into a zombie again."

CHAPTER 13

"**T**HAT'S INSANE!" I SAID, THINKING BACK ON the time Yancy had turned into a zombie in the Overworld. Back when we were still enemies, and not friends. After Yancy had turned into a zombie, he learned he was able to keep his human brain and could order all the normal zombies around. That allowed him to create a zombie army. But right now . . .

I stopped. I realized he was brilliant.

"You're going to turn into a zombie so you can tell all the zombies here to fight against Herobrine and the Overworld armies, aren't you?" I gasped.

"Yancy, that's dangerous!" Destiny said. "It worked before, but what if it doesn't work again? What if you don't keep your mind this time, and you just become a drooling, brainless zombie?"

Yancy looked at her grimly. "I don't think we have much choice here."

"But what about my mom?" Alex said. "I don't want the zombies hurting my mom!"

She had a good point. We needed someone to help us, but could we really trust zombies? Wouldn't they just make things worse by hurting the people of the Overworld? Deep down, these were all good people who wouldn't be acting this way if Herobrine wasn't forcing them!

"I'll take care of that," Yancy promised Alex. "Let me do what I need to do."

He'd caught sight of Dirk and Mitch, still cowering. They'd hidden under a table decorated with orange and black streamers, and they were holding each other and shaking. Somehow they'd managed not to be attacked by any zombies yet, which was a miracle. I had a feeling a lot of other kids must have been helping them.

But most of the other kids had run to the far end of the room, trying to hide from Aunt Alexandra's army. And several zombies had spotted Dirk and Mitch and were closing in on them . . .

"Help us!" Mitch cried as Yancy ran in that direction.

"Yeah, we'll share our candy!" Dirk yelped.

I saw the relief on the bullies' faces as Yancy drew nearer. But when Yancy dove into the pile of zombies like an offering, Dirk and Mitch screamed again and pulled even closer to each other.

The zombies were only too happy to have their meal jump right at them. They sank their rotten teeth into Yancy.

"Now!" I said. Alex, Maison, Destiny, and I rushed in moments later, hitting the zombies with our weapons. We needed Yancy to be bitten, but not seriously hurt. We were able to take the zombies out in just a few moments. Yancy still sprawled there on his hands and knees, gasping and choking for breath.

His hands had already turned green.

Slowly, achingly, Yancy raised himself to his feet and faced us full on. It was difficult not to shudder at his deep green face. Even his eyes had turned a creepy, dark red.

"Z-zombie!" Dirk and Mitch screamed.

"Yancy, did it work?" Destiny asked. She meant: Is that still you in there?

"Yes, it worked!" Yancy said, his voice raspy.

He vaulted up on the table Dirk and Mitch were hiding under, using it like a new stage.

"Zombies!" he shouted.

At once, all the zombies stopped attacking people. They turned their heads toward Yancy. Aunt Alexandra was just releasing her feet from the stage, and I saw her startled look as she realized the zombies were obeying Yancy instead of Herobrine.

"Zombies!" Yancy shouted again. "I am your leader now. I order you to stop the Overworld armies and leave the humans alone! Do not hurt the Overworld armies, and do not turn them into zombies. Just push them back through the portal into the Overworld, and don't let them hurt anyone here!"

I held my breath, waiting to see if it would work.

On cue, the zombies stopped attacking the kids huddled in the dark corners of the room. They turned toward the Overworld army, hissing.

"Stop the zombies!" Aunt Alexandra commanded, yanking her foot loose. She stormed down the stage. Before she could reach us, two zombies lurched in front of her, blocking the way. They began pushing her back toward the portal, only to be cut down by her sword.

Yancy looked at the kids trying to hide in the back. "I need your help!" he shouted. "The zombies will leave you alone now. Take your weapons back up to defend yourselves, and push the Overworld people back through the portal, into the *Minecraft* world!"

Ms. Reid was bringing in another giant load of wooden swords. "Get your swords, kids!" she said. "I have even more in my classroom!"

The kids and the teachers descended on Ms. Reid's box of weapons, grabbing wooden swords and running out to fight. The screams turned to roars as the kids cheered each other on.

My heart gave a thrill of hope. Together, the kids and zombies were pushing the Overworld soldiers back through the portal. No one was getting hurt, but something was being done!

"You're brilliant, Yancy!" I called over the fighting.

Yancy got down from the table, shaking his head. "This is only a small battle in a worldwide fight," he said. He pointed to the movie screen. Herobrine was continuing to show up in the different shots of cities, egging his soldiers on. He seemed so caught up in what he was doing that he wasn't aware of anything else. The more he got worked up over destruction, the more his eyes glowed in a sickly, feverish way.

All my good feelings immediately went away. Yancy was right.

"We need to get the word out!" Maison said. "We need to tell people how to fight and how to protect themselves."

"But I thought you said this world was too big for us to reach everyone!" Alex protested. "What can we do?"

When I saw a look of triumph on Maison's face, I knew she had come up with a great idea. My heart started to pound with newfound hope.

Using her baseball bat, Maison pointed across the room. In the doorway stood a wild-eyed Lilac, her microphone gripped in her hand. Beside her was the cameraman, recording everything that was going on.

CHAPTER 14

WHEN LILAC SAW WE WERE LOOKING AT HER, she began to frantically beckon us over. We raced across the room to her, ducking through zombies and battling Overworld soldiers.

"Do you believe us now?" Destiny called out as we got close.

"Believe you!" Lilac sputtered. "This is the best story I'm going to get in my life! Tell me what's going on! You—you turned into a zombie!" She turned her heavily lashed eyes on Yancy's green skin and red irises, momentarily speechless.

"Zombies and soldiers from the Overworld are attacking people all over Earth!" I said. "We know how people can defend themselves!"

"You have to have this broadcast everywhere," Yancy cut in.

She nodded. "Yes," she said. "Whatever you need. This is live, so start talking!"

The cameraman zeroed his camera in on Yancy and Lilac put her microphone right to his face. I guessed Yancy's whole turning-into-a-zombie-live-on-camera thing got him special attention.

"Zombies!" he shouted. "I need all the zombies out there to hear me! Stop attacking the people on Earth. Leave them alone. Push the soldiers of the Overworld back through the portals, but do not hurt them!"

I looked on the screen, hoping that Yancy's words would get the zombies to stop attacking people. But it wasn't working. All the zombies on the screen were as evil as ever, attacking every person in sight.

Before I could say anything, I saw Lilac was on a cell phone. "I'm getting good stuff!" she said. "Make it so it's not just going live locally—make it go live everywhere! Yes, I'm serious—I saw this boy turn into a zombie and start ordering the zombies around here, and they're obeying him. I don't care what it takes— the whole world needs to see this!"

Maison jumped into the camera's focus with Yancy. "If you play *Minecraft*, this is just like that. Kids of the world, you all play *Minecraft*, right? Teach your parents how to protect themselves. Fight the attacking zombies with any weapons you have, like baseball bats. If you hit them, you can defeat them. The *Minecraft* people coming out of the portals don't mean to hurt you, but Herobrine is controlling them right now."

"This is all connected to the streaming videos of Herobrine," Destiny said. "I know it sounds crazy, but you're seeing it happening before your own eyes! Those Herobrine videos weren't a prank, and he wants to destroy the world for real!"

Lilac clicked off her silvery cell phone. "My boss is working on getting it to go live across the globe," she said.

"Yancy's face is on the screen!" Alex cried, gesturing toward the giant screen.

I couldn't believe it! In one of the city scenes, a big building was seen in the background, and there was Yancy's face on it, talking. "Zombies!" I could hear him say, like a distant echo. "I need all the zombies out there to hear me!"

It worked. All the zombies on that screen stopped attacking. By the time Yancy's little speech was done, they were no longer battling the people of Earth. Instead, they were pushing the Overworld troops back into the nearby portal.

On the screen, the people went stone-still in shock, hardly daring to believe they were no longer under a zombie onslaught. Then Maison's face appeared on the building, telling the people what to do. There were some kids in that city who were dressed up like people from *Minecraft* for Halloween, right down to pretend diamond swords. When they heard Maison's directions, their faces lit up because they understood and knew what they had to do. They began to show the adults how to fight back.

Lilac had one hand over her mouth. "It's really working!" Quick as could be, her cell phone was back out. "Are you seeing this?" she demanded into the phone. "Good, good, keep getting it played!"

In another screen, there was a store nearby the portal with TVs in the window. Those TVs began to play Yancy, and then Maison. The zombies stopped attacking. The people began to defend themselves.

It wasn't all good. I saw Herobrine floating over one of the portals, laughing and jumping through the air. Our news footage must not have aired near there yet, because the zombies were still attacking. And Herobrine seemed totally unaware that we were ruining his plans in other places.

"This is the power of the world wide web and mass communication," Yancy said with pride, though I didn't entirely understand what he meant. He turned back to the camera and said, "Everyone, Herobrine wants to ruin this world because he's seen that people can be cruel, and he thinks we deserve this. He thinks this because he's the cruelest of all, and he doesn't believe anyone can be saved or changed. I want this world to prove him wrong. We need to stop fighting over our differences and come together. We need to stop using the Internet as a place to bully one another or harass people or get outraged over every little thing. We need to use it as a way to spread useful information and help one another!"

"Wow, Yancy!" Destiny said, impressed. "That's inspiring. You need to join speech class!"

"I know I look weird now," Yancy said, laying one green hand over his chest. "And I know I've done things in the past I regret. We've all done things we wish we hadn't. But we always have time to make things better."

"And we have time to defeat Herobrine!" Alex cut in, as if she thought Yancy was starting to sound too sappy and we needed to get everyone pumped up.

"Like Alex said!" Yancy replied. "We can do this!"

More and more zombies on the screen began to change. They were becoming our allies! But as exciting as all this was, there was still something very troubling.

Even if we pushed the people of the Overworld back home, and even if we had the zombies starting to work for us now, that didn't solve the real problem. The only way to really stop all this madness was to beat Herobrine.

We were saying brave words. We were cheering the Earth on.

But we had no idea how we could actually stop Herobrine. And unless we came up with something fast, he would find out what we were up to and come at us with new monsters and new terrors.

CHAPTER 15

I WAS IN A ROOM FILLED WITH NOISES—SLASHING swords and moaning zombies and the thunder of battle. But now my whole body tensed as I heard a very specific noise, a very specific creepy music. It wasn't any old creepy music, either. It was the music from my nightmares about Herobrine. The sound was coming from my toolkit.

The music disc!

I yanked the music disc out so fast that I almost dropped it in my clumsy hands. Lilac had her microphone out and was talking into the camera, but Yancy, Maison, Destiny, and Alex all heard the music disc. We stepped out of the way of the camera, trying to get to a quieter corner of the room.

"The stage is set.
The world turns in the favor of the tyrant.

It will take the work of all to defeat him.
Through teamwork and by conquering fears
the five can become more.
Everything needed to defeat him
is already with you."

And that was it. The music disc went silent again.

I had gotten so excited to hear it speak again, and now I was mad. This prophecy didn't tell us anything! All the prophecies were doing at this point was saying Herobrine could be defeated, and we had to work together, blah, blah, blah, and that the five of us were the key to defeating him. But couldn't the music disc give us some *real* clues? If we had everything we needed to defeat him, what *were* those things?

"It's a riddle!" Alex said angrily. "Earth and the Overworld don't have time for riddles."

"We already have what we need?" Maison looked down at her bat. "How can we have everything we need? When we attacked Herobrine with our weapons before, all it did was make him disappear. We need to do something different this time."

"He was weakened when I shot him with arrows," Alex said. "But I wasn't able to bring him down."

"He was distracted," Yancy said. "Just like he's distracted now. We have to use his arrogance against him."

"So, we distract him and then all five of us attack?" Alex wondered.

"But what is this 'work of all' and 'five can become more'?" Destiny asked, her eyes very serious as she thought.

Alex looked over her shoulder at the movie screen. "I can see where he is, but I have no idea how to get there. I wonder when Yancy's newscast will air where he is."

"Wait!" Destiny said so loudly we all jumped. When we looked back at her, I saw her eyes were glowing as if she was lit up by an incredible idea.

"What is it?" I asked breathlessly.

"I know what we have," Destiny said. "Technology. We have to defeat him using it. And we have to do it fast, before he realizes what's going on."

My heart was pounding. "But what kind of technology?" I demanded. Destiny and Yancy were both great at tech, Maison was pretty good, and Alex and I were pretty clueless since we hadn't grown up around it.

"Yancy!" Destiny said, turning toward him quickly. "Does your *Minecraft* game still work on your phone?"

"Uh . . ." Yancy looked at her expressionlessly for a second, then checked his phone. "Yeah. Why?"

"Herobrine stole into this world using your *Minecraft* game on your cell phone," she said. "It doesn't matter if we know exactly where he is. He can be found in the game. Give everyone in the world your IP address so they can get into your game with you. A multiplayer attack! Tell them to go after Herobrine! That will raise the five—us—to as many people as there are on the Earth. And we have everything we need to defeat him right here!" She pointed to our weapons and Yancy's phone.

"Of course!" Maison said. "He can knock off a few attacks, but if we really can reach people at a global level, we can get millions of people online to attack him at the same time."

"It's the best chance we've got," Yancy said. "Great thinking, Destiny! Even if it doesn't defeat him, it's got to weaken his health. If we get him distracted and weakened . . ."

I realized I was breathing heavily, from both excitement and fear. Yancy threw himself right in front of Lilac and the camera. "What is it?" she asked, seeing from his face that he needed to say something big.

"I might know how to beat Herobrine and make all the portals disappear," Yancy said.

That got Lilac's full attention. Yancy explained the plan and gave his IP address, and within a minute his newscast was starting to show up on some of the cities on the movie screen. Wherever it did show up, I saw people snatching out their phones, tablets, and computers. Kids were showing their parents how to play *Minecraft*.

"It's a worldwide manhunt!" Maison marveled.

We're coming for you, I thought angrily, watching Herobrine on the screen. *We'll find you soon.*

While I was thinking this, Herobrine was still gloating and laughing at the Earth people being attacked by zombies. Then Herobrine stopped laughing. He jerked as if some invisible thing had hurt him. He stumbled, holding his leg where Alex had shot him earlier.

For the first time, that terrible smile left his face. He was no longer gloating.

And Yancy's original newscast must have been playing somewhere nearby Herobrine, because abruptly the zombies stopped attacking the people, and instead began to turn on the soldiers.

"Stop!" Herobrine howled. "Zombies, attack the people!"

The zombies stopped and looked confused. Who was more powerful, Herobrine or Yancy? Most of the zombies began to attack the people again, though a few continued to go after the soldiers. Up close and personal, Herobrine's power over the zombies was stronger than Yancy's. But maybe the fact that some zombies still followed Yancy's directions was a sign that Herobrine was growing weaker?

For a moment I thought Herobrine might have looked afraid, though as quickly as I saw it, the fear was gone from his face. Instead, his expression became consumed with rage.

He emitted a hideous, animal-like roar of fury, the kind of roar that sent chills all over my body. Then he turned to the portal behind him and leapt through it.

I scanned all the scenes on the big movie screen, trying to see if Herobrine would reappear. He didn't, but there were so many more cities under attack that he wasn't showing us. Was he in one of those cities? Had he escaped back to the Overworld?

"Where is he?" I yelped.

A moment later, I got my answer. Herobrine stormed out of the portal onstage, his face twitching, his teeth bared like fangs. The red lights were swirling all over him. The temperature plummeted at his very presence, and his white eyes sought out our group.

"Stevie," he said, his voice a monster's growl. "This is all your doing!"

"It's all of us!" Alex said bravely. "We have the whole world fighting against you!"

Herobrine's form gave a little tremor. "Oh, you think you've won," he said in a sickening voice. "But the battle is far from over."

"Are you getting this?" Lilac called to her cameraman.

"You're acting fearless, but I can see the attacks are weakening your health!" Yancy said. "Surrender now and turn things back to how they were before."

"You're all fools!" Herobrine spat out. "You think some puny attacks will weaken me enough to stop me? Besides, I still have the upper hand."

He reached back into the portal and wrenched out a man from the Overworld. The force of Herobrine's might was still so strong that the man fell weakly forward on his stomach. He lay there a moment, coughing. Herobrine grabbed the man by the back of his head and forced his face up, so we could all see who it was. Even though the man's eyes were clamped shut, I would recognize him from anywhere.

"Dad!" I cried.

"I still have your father, Stevie!" Herobrine shouted. "He's worth more to you than some measly world, isn't he? I'll tell you what: I return your father if you call off the attacks on me. If you don't . . ." He paused to let the horror sink in. "Then your father is mine forever."

"You can't do this!" I tried to run forward, even though I didn't know what I was going to do. I wanted to grab Dad and protect him. Before I could get far, Yancy's hand flew out and he seized me by my sleeve.

"Don't do it, Stevie!" Yancy hissed in a whisper. "He's lying! He's never going to release your dad to us, and if we call off the attacks, we're all doomed!"

I froze. I didn't know what to think. I didn't know what to do.

Herobrine watched me grimly, waiting for my answer. "Fine," he said after a moment. "Then you'll just have to come find me."

He snatched Dad up and jumped through the portal, both of them vanishing off into another world.

CHAPTER 16

"**D**AD!" I CRIED, RUNNING TOWARD THE STAGE. "Dad, come back!"

As if my dad had a choice.

"We have to go through that portal!" Alex said. I realized the others were running beside me, not trying to stop me now.

"But we can't leave everyone here!" Destiny said. "There are still people attacking the students!"

Ms. Reid was standing near the stage, and she stepped in front of me before I could reach it. I came to a screeching halt right before her. What was she thinking? I had to get through that portal!

"Stevie!" she said. "Run, go after your father!" I saw she held a wooden sword in her hand, and she held it high. "I'll watch over everyone here and keep them safe."

"Thank you," I stammered, feeling a sudden rush of gratitude. It was all such a blur. The battle here was mostly over, and with Ms. Reid acting like a general and arming the students with wooden swords, I had faith they would be okay.

"No need to thank me," Ms. Reid said. "Go fight that villain!"

The five of us rushed to the portal, leaping through almost at once. When we fell out on the other side, I realized right away where we were. The portal had taken us to the temple high atop a mountain where we had fought Herobrine before. The mountain was surrounded by forests, but as I looked, all the trees had lost their leaves as far as my eyes could see. It was a sign of Herobrine's presence, all those skeletal trees reaching up to the sky, their branches out as if begging for help.

"Oh no!" I said.

Herobrine was nowhere in sight.

Neither was my dad.

But over the mountain, and across the forests, there were portals. Hundreds upon hundreds of them, with mist rising up from their bottoms, all of them channels to more worlds, more destinations.

Herobrine could have jumped into any one of these with Dad.

How were we ever going to find them?

CHAPTER 17

"**S**HOULD WE SPLIT UP?" MAISON ASKED TENSELY.

"If we split up, we could get lost," Alex said.

That wasn't the only thing worrying me. Down the mountain and in the forest, I could see lots of soldiers from the Overworld. They looked as if they'd been pushed back through the portals from wherever they'd been on Earth. And they were fighting a bunch of weird-looking people. The people looked kind of like Overworld people with square bodies, but a lot of them were shaped like cartoon and comic book characters from Maison's world. They also all had normal eyes instead of Herobrine-blank eyes. I didn't understand.

"Those must be the players jumping onto Yancy's IP to help us out!" Destiny said. "They all have different *Minecraft* skins!"

I realized she had to be right. The weird-looking people weren't trying to hurt the Overworld armies, but they were protecting the portals and making sure the armies didn't go back through them to Earth. I didn't see any soldiers or *Minecraft* players up the mountain, so we kept our attention on what was right in front of us.

"If I were to guess," Yancy said, "I think Herobrine would have gone into a portal someplace where the zombies haven't driven the Overworld soldiers back. So it'd probably be through a portal with no one around it."

That made sense, but it still didn't help much. Even by eliminating the portals with soldiers near them, there were still hundreds of portals without soldiers.

"Should we try one?" Alex said, gesturing to the closest portal to us.

We didn't know what else to do, and standing there wasn't giving us any more clues. When we went through the portal, we arrived in a big Earth city full of skyscrapers. I'd seen pictures of skyscrapers like that, though I'd never seen them in real life. They towered darkly overhead.

"Zombies!" I said.

Zombies and Overworld soldiers were still attacking the people here. People were running for cover and yelling at one another in a language I didn't know. But then one of the skyscrapers lit up on the side, and Yancy's face appeared.

"The newscast is just reaching here!" I said.

As the Yancy on screen talked, I saw writing scrolling underneath his face.

"It's subtitled!" Maison said. "They really are making sure everyone can understand. This is great!"

I didn't know what subtitles meant, but the people here responded to the footage and began to fight back. The zombies also turned against the Overworld soldiers.

"I don't see Herobrine here," I said. "And it looks like the tide is turning in this battle."

We jumped back through the portal. Going into the next portal, we saw almost the same thing. The newscast was reaching the people and helping them defend themselves.

When we were back in the Overworld, I exclaimed, "This isn't working! We can't just keep jumping back through portals!"

Even as I said that, I didn't know what else I could suggest. But if we kept going through portal after portal, that might give Herobrine enough time to hurt Dad and find new ways to fight.

"Stevie?" I heard a frail voice call.

My heart started thumping even harder in my chest. "Dad?" I called back. His voice sounded so weak and unlike him, but I knew it was him! "Dad! Where are you?"

We all looked around, and then I saw him. He was on a ledge a little lower on the mountain, though still very close to the top. It was a small ledge, with no portal on it, and Dad was lying with his face away from us. If he rolled just a little, he'd fall off.

"Dad!" I cried, and began running down to the ledge. Herobrine was nowhere to be seen, as if he'd wounded Dad and just dumped him there to suffer.

How hurt is he? I wondered desperately. Dad wasn't the kind to lie there and cry out for help. He was strong. "Dad, Dad, I'm coming!"

"Stevie, wait!" Yancy called from behind.

I didn't wait. I threw myself down on the ledge, my feet hitting the ground hard. Dad still didn't turn to see me. He must have been really hurt.

"Dad," I said, putting my hand on his shoulder, trying to turn him my way and help him up.

As soon as Dad started to turn, I saw his eyes were still shut and he held his diamond sword in his hand. The sword had been hidden from my sight because of how he'd been lying there. As he moved, he raised his sword, casting a shadow over me.

His eyes popped open.

They were the same blank, white eyes as Herobrine's.

With a roar, Dad lunged at me.

CHAPTER 18

I JUST BARELY DODGED DAD'S SWORD BLOW, AND HIS blade hit the side of the mountain, sticking there. He ripped the sword out of the stone and turned back toward me.

"Stevie!" Maison cried. She skidded down the mountain and landed on the ledge, the others right behind her. They all crowded around me like a shield as Dad loomed, stalking closer to us. If we backed up only a few inches, we'd fall off the ledge to the ground far below.

There was a terrible laughing overhead.

Herobrine stood on one ledge just above us, bellowing with laughter. "You fools!" he shouted hoarsely. "Of course he's still working for me! I only had him play sick and weak to trick you!"

Dad lunged toward us with his sword. I threw my sword out to halt him and the others tried to push him back with their weapons without hurting him.

"I told you before, Stevie, that I chose your father to be second-in-command of my armies!" Herobrine continued. "He is powerless against me and will do whatever I ask. I had him leading zombies and Overworld armies just as I had Alexandra doing, but I didn't let you see because I had a feeling I could pull this trick on you. Oh, the look on your face when you realized!"

Now Herobrine shouted to Dad, "Steve!"

Like an obedient toy, Dad stopped and waited for his command.

"Finish them off," Herobrine said, crossing his arms. "All five of them. This time, I'm sticking around to make sure the job is finished."

Dad struck out at us with a sword again while Herobrine watched from his perch, as entertained as someone watching TV in Maison's world.

"It's still five against one," Alex said, yanking up her bow. "We can still stop him." But a moment later, she cried out in shock. An arrow had flown out of nowhere, taking Alex's out before she could send it flying.

Where had that arrow come from? I pushed back at Dad's sword and got a glimpse above. Aunt Alexandra was now next to Herobrine on his ledge, her bow still raised.

"Mom!" Alex yelped.

"You're not the only one who knows archery, little girl," Aunt Alexandra hissed. She shot another arrow, this time straight at Alex. Alex dove to the ground to save herself and almost got trampled by Dad's big feet.

With a graceful gesture, Aunt Alexandra vaulted down to join us on our ledge. As soon as she landed, she lifted her bow again. Maison ran at her, hitting the bow back with her bat, momentarily stalling Aunt Alexandra.

Alex jumped back up to her feet, spitfire mad. "Herobrine!" she thundered. "Get down here and fight us yourself!"

"Why?" Herobrine asked. "I'm rather enjoying this family get-together."

"You're acting tough, but you don't fool us!" Alex went on. "If you were strong enough, you'd be down here fighting, too. You're having other people do your work for you because you've been weakened by all the attacks on the *Minecraft* game!"

I suddenly realized what Alex was doing. If Herobrine was overhead and we were being attacked by Dad and Aunt Alexandra, we didn't have the ability to attack him. If we at least got him on this ledge with us, we might have a chance, however small.

Herobrine snorted with contempt. "Is that what you think?"

He disappeared and then reappeared on the ledge. Even though he'd come down to our level, he'd purposefully put himself at the best spot of the ledge. He was right up against the mountain, nowhere close enough to the edge to fall off. On top of that, both

Dad and Aunt Alexandra were standing in front of him, so we'd have to get past them first. He was still letting others do his work for him.

"Well, here I am," Herobrine said. He twitched. "And somehow I feel as safe as ever."

He's not totally safe! I thought. I could see that he was still getting weaker. His posture wasn't as good. But he was still pretty strong, and with Dad and Aunt Alexandra working as his guards . . .

With a grunt, Dad hurled his sword at me. I blocked, ducked under him, tried to get away. The end of the ledge was inches from me, and I could almost feel it like a vacuum, the gravity wanting to pull me down.

Think, think! This has to be it—there has to be a way to defeat him. He's weakened . . . his zombies are turning against him . . . people are getting wise about how to fight him. But how to end it?

"I also have power over the Overworld, the Nether, and now Earth as well," I remember Herobrine saying earlier.

And then it hit me.

The Overworld, the Nether, and Earth. His powers snaked through all those places, keeping him a step above us.

But there was one world left that he hadn't mentioned having power in.

That was how we had to end it. We had to take him to the End, the scariest world of all. A world of eternal night, a world I'd never been to—a world no one I knew had ever been to, not even my brave dad.

In the End, you found yourself on an island in the sky, and if you fell off, you fell forever. Endermen walked the land, and the Ender Dragon flew through the dark sky. The story was that if you conquered the Ender Dragon, you would return home.

In fact, there was no other way to go home from the End.

If we took Herobrine there, it might be the end for him. But it would also be the end for anyone who went with him.

CHAPTER 19

MUST BE CRAZY! I THOUGHT RIGHT AWAY. THERE WAS no way we could go to the End, not with all the danger it entailed.

Besides, it was basically impossible to make a portal to the End. Regular portals like the ones to the Nether wouldn't work. You needed all these ingredients that were hard to get at a regular time, let alone when you were trapped on a ledge!

But then it hit me again.

Yancy's cell phone!

We couldn't get all the ingredients together to make a portal here, but Yancy or Destiny probably knew a way to make it on the *Minecraft* game on their cell phones by using codes for a shortcut. How could I tell them to make it without Herobrine overhearing, though?

I was so deep in my thoughts that I didn't fully dodge Dad's next blow. I managed to get out of the way of his blade, but the sword handle still thunked hard against my shoulder, knocking me to the ground. Dad towered above me and raised his sword.

As I tried to scramble to my feet, Maison jumped between Dad and me, slashing out with her bat. The first slash she made stopped Dad's sword. Then she swung again, pushing him back a little.

In the same instant, Destiny rushed to my side, grabbed me under my arms, and started pulling me up. "Stevie, I've got you!" she said.

"The End," I whispered. It was too risky to say any more. If I went into a whole discussion of what I thought we needed to do, Herobrine would hear for sure.

Destiny's eyebrows flew up and her mouth fell open. She seemed to understand.

Near the back of the ledge, Herobrine chuckled. "Ready to give up, Stevie?" he said.

"Distract him," Destiny whispered back, and released me. I dove forward, past where Dad and Maison were fighting. Out of the corner of my eye I saw Destiny run to Yancy, reach into his pocket, and yank out the cell phone. Yancy, who was helping Alex keep Aunt Alexandra at bay, was startled by having his cell phone snatched and looked at Destiny in surprise. Destiny didn't say a word; her thumbs were going crazy tapping something into the phone.

Right before I was about to reach Herobrine, Dad grabbed me. In his other hand he held Maison's arm so hard that he'd made her drop her bat. Maison was kicking at him, but Herobrine's power seemed so strong that Dad didn't even feel it.

"Well, it looks as though I have the two of you caught," Herobrine said. "Once I get you twerps out of the way, I can go back to destroying the worlds."

"What about what you said earlier?" I asked. "That you'd let my dad go if we called off the attacks?"

"What, that?" Herobrine said. "Did you really believe I'd make a bargain like that? I only wanted the attacks called off. I'd never give your father back, Stevie, and you know it."

I struggled against Dad's grip, but he held me tight.

"What shall I do with them, master?" Dad asked.

"Throw them off the ledge," Herobrine said. "That should take care of things."

Dad started to turn toward the edge, and Maison and I struggled to get free. Herobrine watched, his eyes glowing with anticipation.

Destiny, hurry up! I thought. I didn't know how long it would take her to make a portal to the End, but we didn't exactly have time to spare here.

"What's this?!" Herobrine suddenly shouted, sounding outraged.

I looked back. Somehow Alex had managed to cover her mom's boots with arrows again, pinning her without actually hurting her.

"Don't just stand there!" Herobrine ordered Dad. "Help her get free, then take care of those brats! I need both of you!"

Dad's grip on Maison and me started to loosen as he turned toward Aunt Alexandra.

Behind Herobrine, I saw a shape take form against the hard rock of the mountainside. It was a green-patterned portal, with the inside black as night, little pinpricks showing like stars.

The End portal!

As soon as Dad fully let go, I lunged forward and knocked Herobrine back—into the portal.

CHAPTER 20

MY FIRST GLIMPSE OF THE END WAS A DARK, twilit sky. The island we landed on was made of greenish-white stones, and around the edges of it I could see Endermen, who were tall, skinny mobs with black bodies and long arms and legs.

Herobrine scrambled to his feet, inches away from me. "What did you do?" he hollered. "Coming here condemns us both, boy!"

"I won't let you destroy the worlds!" I said. "I can't stand back and watch you take away everything I love!"

In this already dark world, something even darker flew over us, casting the island in deep black shadows. When I looked up, I saw the enormous and powerful Ender Dragon soaring through the sky. It didn't seem to have spotted us yet, and I didn't want to be around when it did.

Herobrine stared at me for a moment, his mouth hanging open, and then he began to laugh again. Not expecting this, I twitched. It was a morbid laugh, not his usual, gloating one.

"You've lost everything you love, anyway!" he said. "You'll never see your family or your friends again. You sacrificed yourself and everything you had for an eternity trapped here. Are you proud?"

I didn't have time to answer. The next thing I knew, someone else was coming through the portal.

I jumped back, sword up, wondering if Herobrine had called one of his soldiers in to attack me. First I saw the person's feet, and then their whole body followed. I couldn't believe my eyes. This wasn't someone here to attack me and try to free Herobrine—it was Alex!

"Alex!" I said. "You didn't need to come here, too! It's dangerous!"

"You think I don't know that?" asked Alex, who loved danger. "We started this mission together, and we're going to finish it together."

My eyes widened as Maison, Destiny, and Yancy jumped through the portal, too.

"Stevie, you're okay!" Maison said. She'd grabbed her baseball bat again, and she held it at the ready.

"You guys didn't all have to come," I said.

"Of course we did," Maison said. "We wouldn't leave you, Stevie!"

"We're not going to leave behind one of our friends," Yancy said.

The five of us turned our eyes on Herobrine.

"You're all fools!" Herobrine was shouting. He looked as if he wanted to throw a tantrum. "There's no portal out of the End! It's insanity enough that one of you would willingly come here, but all five!"

"This is your prison, Herobrine," Yancy said. "You can't get out of here."

Herobrine's eyes filled with a hideous, revolting desperation. He pointed one arm viciously my way. "Well, you're getting what you want, aren't you, Stevie?" he said. "You offered to be my prisoner if I let the others go. Now you're imprisoned here with me. But as long as I'm around, the portals stay open. Other mobs will find their way through those portals and attack. The people of the Overworld will remain brainwashed. There will be eternal suffering because of me, and I welcome that!"

The Endermen at the edges of the island had noticed us and started to creep forward, curious.

"You don't have any weapons, Herobrine!" I said. "Surrender and take away your dark magic!"

"Never!" Herobrine charged toward us, screaming. He was going to try to push us off the island, into the infinity below!

We bolted out of the way, but as I turned, Herobrine grabbed my foot. I fell on my stomach, emitting an "Oof!"

Herobrine was trying to drag me off the edge.

"I'll throw you from here and feed you to the Ender Dragon!" Herobrine boomed.

Immediately the others began jumping on him, hitting him with all their weapons, trying to get him to release me. Herobrine shook them off like a dog, sending them flying all around him.

The Endermen came closer and closer. Suddenly one was right next to Herobrine, its head looming over him. Endermen are twice as tall as people from the Overworld, and Herobrine looked small and vulnerable next to this one.

"Stop it!" Herobrine ordered. He let go of me and I hurried away.

The Endermen didn't stop. They kept popping up all around Herobrine, staring at him in fascination. They'd never seen anything like him before. When he lashed out at them, he didn't seem as strong as he had only moments before. He was panting.

I gripped my sword and stood with the others. Herobrine managed to break free of the Endermen, charging toward us. His hand came out to grab me. I thrust my sword at him at the same time the others threw out their weapons in defense. Herobrine teetered, then fell back against the Endermen. He pushed the Enderman he'd fallen into, but he was on the edge of the island now, his feet unsteady with loss of health.

"I'll take you all out!" he screamed, his eyes burning like lightning.

When he charged again, he ran straight into an Enderman. "No!" he cried, realizing what he'd done to himself. His foot slipped, and he fell back from the island, plummeting down into the darkness below.

CHAPTER 21

WE ALL CROWDED AROUND THE EDGE, WATCHing Herobrine fall until he couldn't be seen anymore.

"Is he gone?" I asked, trembling.

"Look out!" Alex said.

Now that the Endermen had lost Herobrine, they were interested in us, and they hurried our way. I thrust my sword up at one to protect myself, but more were coming, and then we were surrounded. The Endermen towered overhead, reaching for us. And then something snatched us back.

The next thing we knew, Maison, Alex, Yancy, Destiny, and I had been transported back to the top of the mountain, by the temple. All around us the forests had regained their leaves. The portals were shattering, one by one, exploding as if they'd never been there to begin with. The players in the *Minecraft* skins were also disappearing.

"What happened?" I said, shocked. When I'd decided to take Herobrine to the End, I'd thought I'd never see the Overworld again.

"We must have defeated Herobrine with that fall!" Maison said.

"But we have to defeat the Ender Dragon to return to the Overworld from the End," I said, thinking about its terrifying form flying over us. "And it never came near!"

"It must be because we defeated such a powerful mob, so it worked like defeating the Ender Dragon!" Yancy said.

All throughout the mountainside and down below I could see the soldiers of the Overworld. They were scratching their heads and looking around in confusion as if they'd just woken up from a deep sleep. All of their eyes were back to normal.

Destiny still had Yancy's cell phone, and she exclaimed, "The news!"

There was Lilac Waters on the phone screen, reporting from the middle school Halloween party. In the background I couldn't see any zombies or Overworld soldiers. And the portal was gone!

"Minutes ago, something amazing happened here," Lilac was saying. "All the zombies and soldiers vanished at the same time that the portal on this stage exploded. Now I'm getting reports that the same thing is happening all over the globe. People who were playing *Minecraft* to help are also reporting that they were knocked out of the game the same moment. We did it, planet Earth."

In the background, Dirk and Mitch could be seen sliding out from under the table where they'd been cowering.

"I think we're safe, Mitch," Dirk asked.

"Let's never dress up as zombies again, Dirk," Mitch said. "I've seen enough zombies to last a lifetime."

"Let's speak to the teacher who heroically saved the day here," Lilac said, pulling Ms. Reid in front of the camera. Ms. Reid gave the camera an exhausted smile and held up a wooden sword.

"The great work here comes from our impressive student body," Ms. Reid said. "The students all banded together."

"It seems the whole world banded together," Lilac said. "Wouldn't you agree?"

"It would seem so," Ms. Reid said. "But I only did what I had to do to protect my students here. I want us all to realize how much a young group of kids helped us. Stevie, Maison, Destiny, wherever you are, we thank you. I also want to thank the young girl with red hair who was with them, and the young man who turned into a zombie."

"Aw, she doesn't know our names," Yancy said to Alex, sounding a little disappointed.

"That's okay," Alex said. "What really mattered is defeating Herobrine. Besides . . ." She gave a flip of her red hair toward Yancy. "When you get back to Earth, you have plenty to time to tell everyone our names."

As exciting as all this was, there was something else we needed to do. "Dad!" I called. "Aunt Alexandra!"

And I heard Dad's voice call back, "Stevie? Stevie! We're down here on a ledge!"

Alex and I raced to the edge of the mountain. When we peered down, we could see Aunt Alexandra and Dad, still on the ledge where we'd left them. Aunt Alexandra had freed her feet from Alex's arrows, and the two of them were looking up at us with frantic, worried eyes. Eyes with pupils. Their real eyes.

"Dad!" I cried in relief, and hopped down to be with him.

CHAPTER 22

YANCY TAPPED HIS GLASS OF WATER WITH A spoon, wanting to get everyone's attention. "I think we should have a toast," he said.

"What's a toast?" Alex asked.

Several days later, after the infamous Halloween party, we were at another party. Only this time the people attending were Dad, Aunt Alexandra, Alex, Maison, Destiny, and Yancy—who was back to normal now, thanks to a Potion of Weakness and golden apple I'd made for him after we'd overcome Herobrine. We were all seated at the table in Dad's grand dining room. The table was full of delicious foods from both the Overworld and Earth. This was going to give Maison, Destiny, and Yancy a chance to taste our world's best foods while we got to try theirs. My cat, Ossie, was sitting underfoot, hoping to eat any scraps that fell.

"A toast is something we do on Earth to celebrate," Yancy said. "I propose a toast to a universe free of Herobrine! Raise your glasses with me and clink them together!"

It seemed like a weird ceremony, but we all did it. Dad, Aunt Alexandra, Alex, and I tapped our glasses together slowly, shooting each other Am-I-Doing-This-Right? looks. Yancy, Maison, and Destiny basically slammed their glasses together in triumph. It was a good thing those glasses didn't break, because otherwise we'd have water all over our good food.

"It's amazing what you kids did," Dad was saying as he began to eat. He almost looked choked up about it, which wasn't like Dad.

"Thankfully, defeating Herobrine took care of everything else," Maison said. "As soon as he was defeated, the zombies vanished off Earth, and all the people of the Overworld were teleported back home, safe and sound, with their memories back. All the people on Earth who were turned into zombies immediately turned back into themselves, too." I saw her slip Ossie some fish under the table. Ossie ate eagerly, purring.

"Ms. Reid is going to win a Teacher of the Year award for protecting her students," Destiny said happily. "And I hear Lilac Waters is supposed to be winning a bunch of big journalism awards, too, for her broadcast. I saw her when we got back to Earth, and she said her boss was never going to second-guess her opinions on what stories to cover again!"

"It's so good to have you back, Mom," Alex said, snuggling up against her mom in a sideways hug. Aunt Alexandra put one arm around Alex.

"It was torture," Aunt Alexandra said. "Herobrine had us under his spell, but we retained our minds the whole time."

"You mean . . . ?" I said.

Dad nodded grimly. "We had our minds, but we couldn't move our bodies of our own free will. Inside my brain I was screaming at myself not to hurt you. However, at the same time, Herobrine was making our bodies and mouths move. He had me saying and doing the most terrible things, and attacking you. He knew that would make things all the more painful."

I was shaken by this. "His evil went so deep," I whispered.

"That may be, but he's gone for good now," Yancy said, swishing his drink around and almost spilling more water.

Aunt Alexandra stood up, raising her glass. "I'd like to propose a toast as well. This is how you do it, right?"

Yancy nodded.

"I would like to make a toast to you remarkable kids," she said. "The five of you stuck together through thick and thin. Yancy, Maison, and Destiny, even though you are from another world, I'd like to make you honorary citizens of the Overworld. You are welcome to come visit any time you'd like."

There was a chorus of excited thank-yous.

"There's something else I also want to share with you," Yancy said when we were almost done with our meal. "I brought dessert."

He had his backpack next to him, and now he dumped its contents all over the table.

"This is . . . ?" Dad said, picking up a chocolate candy bar and looking at it with suspicion.

"I won the Halloween party contest for best costume!" Yancy said. "And I'd like to share my winnings with you."

"You won the costume contest as a surly teenager?" I said, confused.

Yancy laughed. "No, I won for being the school's best zombie," he said. "My zombie 'costume' was way more convincing than Dirk and Mitch's, but I still shared some of my candy with them."

Dad took a bite of the chocolate candy bar. "Hmm," he said. "It's good. How do you make it?"

"Uh . . ." Yancy said. I could see he had no idea how people made chocolate bars. Dad still didn't understand how people on Earth didn't make everything themselves.

It didn't matter, though. I looked around the table and thought about how these were my favorite people in the world. My favorite people in any world. Herobrine had brought out the darkness that was possible in the world, but he'd also made us appreciate the light and goodness that was there, too. It made us all more aware of how important friends, family, and kindness were.

I stood and held up my glass. "I'd like to propose a toast, too," I said. "To many more years of friendship."

"And adventure," Alex cut in.

"And adventure," I said.

"I think we can all toast to that," Maison said.

We all clanged our glasses together, cheering.

Check out the rest of the
Unofficial Overworld Adventure series
to find out what happens to Stevie, Alex, and their friends!

Escape from the
Overworld
Danica Davidson

Attack on the
Overworld
Danica Davidson

The Rise of
Herobrine
Danica Davidson

Down into the
Nether
Danica Davidson

The Armies of
Herobrine
Danica Davidson

Battle with the
Wither
Danica Davidson

Available wherever books are sold!